Emma Thomson's

felicity Wishes®

Clutter Clean-Out

and other stories

Hodder
Children's
Books

A division of Hodder Headline Limited

How to make your felicity Wishes.

W I S H

With this book comes an extra special wish for you and your best friend.

Hold the book together at each end and both close your eyes.

Wriggle your noses and think of a number under ten.

Open your eyes, whisper the numbers you thought of to each other.

Add these numbers together. This is your

☆ Magic Number ☆

you

best friend

Place your little finger on the stars, and say your magic number out loud together. Now make your wish quietly to yourselves. And maybe, one day, your wish might just come true. Love

felicity

x

Especially for Emily Jane Ryan
with a special wish for your dreams to come true
E. V. T

Emma Thomson's
felicity Wishes®

FELICITY WISHES
Felicity Wishes © 2000 Emma Thomson
Licensed by White Lion Publishing

Text and Illustrations © 2004 Emma Thomson

First published in Great Britain in 2004 by Hodder Children's Books

A Catalogue record for this book is available from the British Library

ISBN 0 340 88238 7

Printed and bound in Great Britain by Bookmarque Ltd, Croydon, Surrey

The paper and board used in this paperback by Hodder Children's Books are natural recyclable
products made from wood grown in sustainable forests. The manufacturing processes
conform to the environmental regulations of the country of origin.

Hodder Children's Books
A division of Hodder Headline Ltd, 338 Euston Road, London NW1 3BH

CONTENTS

River Rescue

With jammy fingers, Felicity Wishes
brushed her hair out of her eyes.

"It's hard work making picnics!"
said Felicity to her friend Polly.

"But fun!" said Polly, taking a
damp cloth and wiping the jam off
Felicity's nose.

It was Saturday, no fairy school!
Felicity and her three fairy friends,
Holly, Daisy and Polly, had decided
to go on a picnic. Holly had
volunteered to bring the rug, cups

and plates, Daisy was in charge of bringing something yummy to drink, and Polly and Felicity were making the sandwiches and snacks.

"I think I'm nearly done!" said Felicity, standing back and admiring her jam sandwich mountain.

"My cheesy puffs will be ready soon," said Polly, looking at the clock on the cooker. "We've just got time to fly to the apple tree and pick some fruit, and our picnic will be complete!" The fairies raced each other to the orchard at the bottom of the garden.

When they turned up at Holly's house they thought she had forgotten all about their plans.

"Sorry to keep you waiting," said Holly when she eventually opened her front door. "I was having a colour co-ordinating dilemma."

Felicity and Polly raised their eyebrows.

"I just can't decide between the green checked rug and the yellow daisy design plates, or the pink rose rug and the blue spotty plates," she explained. "Come and see!"

The fairy friends followed Holly through the house and out into her back garden. They were used to Holly having this sort of dramatic dilemma.

"There's no choice!" said Felicity,
looking down at both sets laid out
side by side.

"It has to be the pink rose rug.
When in doubt, choose pink!" she
said, because pink was her favourite
colour.

* * *

With heavy bags weighing them down, Holly, Polly and Felicity reached Daisy's house. She was already waiting outside on her front steps.

"Where shall we go?" said Daisy, flying up to meet them.

"I don't know, let's flutter around for a bit until we see somewhere nice," suggested Polly.

"I'm not flying too far with this heavy bag!" said Holly. "Let's go up really high so we can see the whole of Little Blossoming and Bloomfield and choose from there."

"Yeah!" they all agreed excitedly.

It was Polly who spotted a place they'd never been before.

"Look!" she said, "Down there,"

and she pointed to a twinkly blue
thread of water winding in
and out of the dip of
the hills.

"It looks like a magical river," said
Felicity dreamily. "You can see it
glisten as the sunlight catches its
surface."

* * *

The river was just as wonderful as it
had looked from the sky.
On either side of its
banks tall plants
gave shade to tiny
schools of fish.
Lily pads broke
the surface
with heavy
flowers in
pinks and
whites,
and a
small
waterfall
at the top
made a
beautiful,
twinkling sound.
"This is bliss!" said Felicity lying
back in her pink dress on the pink
rose rug, munching happily on
a raspberry jam sandwich.

"It's beautiful!' said Holly, who was down at the water's edge, gazing at her reflection.

"Just lovely!" agreed Polly, who had already thrown off her tights and shoes and was sploshing her feet in the water.

"It's also incredibly interesting!" said Daisy. She wanted to be a Blossom Fairy one day, and had brought along her flower book so that she could identify anything she might not recognise.

"Look at this lily pad," she called, pointing. "It's so magical it moves all by itself."

Felicity knelt down beside her. "You're right! It is moving all by itself!"

"Let me see!" said Polly, jumping up

with a start. As she
swung her feet out of the water
with a huge splosh, the lily pad
jumped up in the air!

"Aghh!" squealed Daisy, as she lost
her balance and fell into the water.

"I'll save you!" said Felicity,
throwing off her shoes.

"It's not deep, just wet!" said Daisy
laughing as she stood up, knee-deep.

"Look!" said Holly, springing to her
feet and pointing with a squeal. "It's
not a magical lily pad – it's a frog!"

All the fairy friends watched in awe
as a little

green

frog

hopped

from one

large leaf to

another.

"I've never seen a frog in real life before," said Felicity.

"I don't expect he's ever seen a fairy!" said Holly.

"I wonder," mused Felicity, as she helped Daisy out of the water, "if he'd like to make friends?"

With Daisy safely on dry land, Felicity set about making her acquaintance with the little green frog.

By the end of the afternoon the little frog and Felicity were inseparable.

"I don't want it to be time to go home already," said Felicity glumly. "It's been the most perfect day. I couldn't eat another jam sandwich if I tried."

"We can always come another day, now we've found this magical spot," said Polly practically.

"Let's make it our secret picnic place!" said Holly.

"I need to come back and finish my notes," said Daisy, putting the lid back on her pen. "There are so many flowers here that I've never seen before."

"I don't want it to be too long before I see my new frog friend again," said Felicity. "Let's make a promise to come back here soon." And all the fairy friends agreed.

As they flew off Felicity turned to wave to the frog. Knowing that they would be coming back again one day made it easier to leave.

"See you soon!" she called.

* * *

The following weeks were hectic, leaving no time for a visit. In ballet class Felicity thought of her new friend so much, it was all she could do to stop herself from leap-frogging! Her school homework book became  covered in doodles and drawings of her green friend and on more than one occasion the blue sky outside the classroom window had turned into the blue river of the little frog's home. The teacher had had to clap sharply to bring her attention back to class.

Finally a day was free for the four fairies to return to their secret magical spot. As they landed, the fairies flopped down on the soft grass, out of breath.

"I've never flown so fast before!" said Felicity panting.

"Me neither," agreed Holly. "My hair must look dreadful!"

"Are you sure this is the spot?" said Daisy, sitting up.

Slowly they looked around. All about them was rubbish. Sweet wrappers, hair-spray cans, old bicycle tyres, paper, bits of wood...

Polly checked her map. "This is definitely where we had our picnic," she said.

"It can't be!" said Daisy, jumping up and walking over to the water's edge. "Look at the river. Our secret picnic spot was full of beautiful unusual flowers, not old tin cans."

Tears sprang to Felicity's eyes. "And if this *is* the spot, then where's the little green frog? I can't see him anywhere."

"It looks as though our secret spot isn't secret any more and your frog friend has moved. There have been an awful lot of picnics here since ours, and not everyone has been as good as us in taking their rubbish away with them," said Polly, picking up the discarded wrapper of a chocolate Twinkle bar.

"That's dreadful," said Felicity. "This was his home."

"There's only one thing I can suggest," said Polly, practical as always. "We clear the rubbish up ourselves and recycle what we can."

Holly looked aghast. "It would take

forever! There's mountains of rubbish and I don't have any rubber gloves!"

"Then let's go to Fairy Godmother and get help," said Felicity urgently. And as fast as they had flown there, the fairies returned home.

✳ ✳ ✳

At school they stood side by side in Fairy Godmother's office and explained what had happened. The next day in assembly there was a special announcement.

"Now, fairies," boomed Fairy Godmother, "today there will be no classes."

Excited squeals and gasps echoed round the hall.

"Quiet please!" she said as she tapped her wand sharply on her lectern. "You already all know how important for our environment it is to be mindful when disposing of your rubbish. Unfortunately, it appears that some fairies have been forgetful and, as a result, areas of great natural beauty are being threatened with becoming common dumping grounds."

Fairy Godmother paused.

"Today is going to be a 'Green Day'. On the notice boards you will see that each House will be dedicated to a special clean-up task. Miss Meandering will be by the front gates with all the equipment you will need and instructions for where you have been assigned to go. Enjoy your day and thank you. Dismissed."

There were three Houses at the
School of Nine Wishes: Hearts, Stars
and Flowers. Felicity was in Hearts,
Holly and Polly were in Stars and
Daisy was in Flowers. Felicity found
her friends in the queue leading
down to the gates.

"It's so exciting!"
she beamed. "When Fairy Godmother
said she would see what she could do,
I never imagined this!"

"Me neither!" said Daisy. "Flowers
are in charge of collecting paper and

plastic for recycling. What are Hearts doing?"

"I'm not sure," said Felicity. "I was in such a rush to find you all I didn't look at the notice board. What about Stars?" she asked, turning to Polly and Holly.

"We've got to collect tin and metal to take to the special melt-down factory so it can be re-used."

"And Miss Meandering is giving us extra special thick gloves!" said Holly happily.

The four fairy friends were delighted to be told that they would all be working in the same area, their special picnic spot. Each was given their Green Clean-up Pack.

"I've got Wellington boots and rubber gloves in mine!" said Felicity, peeping inside the pack as they flew. "Whatever can Hearts House be doing? I really should have checked before I left."

∗ ∗ ∗

When they reached the side of the river Felicity realised exactly what the Wellington boots were for. Dozens of fairies were wading knee-deep in the water, emptying rubbish on to the bank for the Star House fairies and the Flower House fairies to sort into recycling piles.

 By the end of the
day the secret magical picnic spot

looked almost as it had done the very first time the four fairy friends had ever set eyes on it.

All the other fairies from the School of Nine Wishes had left and only Holly, Polly, Daisy and Felicity sat exhausted by the side of the river.

"I found so many old hair-spray cans and make-up jars today that it's really made me think," said Holly. "I'm definitely going to start using refillable bottles."

"I found an old bicycle!" said Polly. "It only needs new tyres and a lick of paint and I'm going to recycle it for myself!"

"A recycled bicycle!" Daisy joked. "The best thing I found today was a beautiful single water lily. It's amazing it managed to survive buried under all those crisp packets." Daisy pointed to the delicate flower alone in the water.

"Look!" said Polly squealing. "It's not just the only surviving water lily, it's also the only surviving jumping water lily!"

Felicity quickly stood up and rushed to the edge.

All the fairies watched with mouths open as the lily bounced and splashed against the surface of the water.

"The little frog!" gasped Felicity, jumping up and down herself.

She quickly pulled on her wellies and splashed into the river. The frog sprang out from under the pad and on to her hand.

"Welcome home and happy Green Day!" she said to her green friend, who almost looked as if he was smiling a little green frog smile!

Take care of
everything around you

for a better
fairy world

Seed Surprise

A small black
spider crawled out from under a large
leaf and Felicity Wishes squealed.

"Argh! Daisy! Help!" she cried.

Felicity was not exactly a fan of
spiders. It wasn't that she held
anything against them personally,
she just didn't like to look at them
for too long. She was never sure how
they did it, but they frightened her.
A lot.

Daisy and Felicity were shopping
at Roots 'n' Shoots, the large garden
nursery in Little Blossoming where
both fairies lived.

"Spider!" she
called from the safety
of the greenhouse ceiling.
Daisy flew up to comfort her.

"Where?" she asked softly.

With wings quivering, Felicity
pointed to the spot.

Daisy quite liked spiders. She was
well aware of all the good things
spiders do to keep the garden
running smoothly. She had tried to
explain to Felicity on several
occasions what wonderful creatures
they were. But it seemed even talking
about spiders made

Felicity's wings
wobble.

"You're safe
to come
down now,"
called Daisy
as she gently
scooped the

spider up in her hands and brushed him outside.

"I'd do a lot more gardening if it wasn't for creepy-crawlies," said Felicity, landing beside her friend.

"Well, maybe that's just it," said Daisy, having a brain-wave. "Perhaps if you did more gardening you'd get used to the creepy-crawlies and not be so scared."

"Hmm," said Felicity, unconvinced.

"Come on, why don't we do it together? I'd like to make my garden more organic."

Unlike Daisy, Felicity just couldn't get excited about getting her wand dirty.

"I suppose…" said Felicity, trying not to offend her friend.

Daisy knew the way to her friend's heart was the colour pink.

"We could grow organic strawberries, and when

they're ripe we can make our very own strawberry milkshake!"

At the thought of strawberry milkshake, Felicity suddenly perked up.

"What are we waiting for?" she said, dashing off towards the seed section. "We've got an organic fruit and vegetable garden to grow!"

* * *

By the time they had got the seeds and flown back to Daisy's house, Felicity was even more excited than Daisy at the prospect of tending to an organic garden. She had forgotten all about being scared of creepy-crawlies.

Daisy made homemade lemonade  while Felicity emptied their morning's shopping on the table. There were seeds of every description. Strawberries, raspberries, blackberries, blueberries, carrots, courgettes, peas and potatoes...

"Where do we start?" sighed Felicity. "There are so many of them."

Just then Holly and Polly, Felicity's two other fairy friends, peeped their heads around the corner of the greenhouse.

"Fancy going to Sparkles for a milkshake?" they called, as they made their way over to Daisy and Felicity.

"Sounds lovely, but Daisy's just made lemonade and we're in the middle of sorting out all these."

Pointing to the seed packets, Felicity told her friends all about their plans for the organic garden.

When she had explained, both Holly and Polly were equally excited and had already picked out the seeds they wanted to help plant.

* * *

Polly wanted to be a Tooth Fairy when she graduated from the School of Nine Wishes, and loved everything toothy, whether it was beaming smiles, magical toothbrushes or minty flavours. She was delighted when she found a seed packet for peppermint and spearmint amongst the dozens that showered the table.

"I'm going to grow these, and when the leaves are mature I can make all sorts of minty things!" she beamed, waggling the packets in her hand. "Just think: mint tea, mint toothpaste, mint perfume."

"Mint perfume?!" her friends repeated.

"Hmm," said Polly with her eyes closed, smiling. "I can smell it now! Don't worry, I'll make enough so that we can all have some."

Holly coughed, trying to stifle her giggles. "I don't mind what I plant," she said, "as long as I don't get dirty."

"You can borrow one of my gardening aprons," offered Daisy.

"Well, only if it matches my crown," said Holly, who was always very conscious of how she looked.

"I'm going to plant all these!" said Felicity enthusiastically, holding up a handful of packets. "I couldn't decide which to choose and then thought I might as well just plant all the pink ones!"

"Then I'll plant the rest," said
Daisy, who loved all plants equally,
"and if we're to get finished before
dark we'd better start right now."

* * *

Each fairy worked on a special plot
to plant their seeds.

"I find the best way to sow is to
make a shallow row with the end of
your wand," said Daisy, showing the
other fairies how it was done.

"And then, very carefully," she
continued, "you can place each seed
so that it nestles right in the centre,
and then gently cover it back over
with earth."

After making her rows,
Felicity picked up the first
of her seed packets. She
was so busy looking at the
picture of the beautiful
strawberry on the front that
when she tore off the top, all
the seeds scattered across the earth!

"Oh goodness," she muttered to
herself, scrambling to try to pick them
up before anyone saw what had
happened. Suddenly Daisy appeared
over Felicity's shoulder.

"How are you getting on?" she
asked.

"Oh, you know," said Felicity,
frantically smoothing the earth over
with the end of her wand and burying
the spilt seeds. "My little rows weren't
even enough and I'm just going to
re-do them before I plant the
strawberries."

"It's very important to give seeds

enough space to grow," said Daisy knowledgeably as she wandered off to the greenhouse.

But Felicity wasn't listening; she was already making plans for a second attempt. After making some new rows in the same place, she set about choosing another packet of seeds.

Felicity used all her concentration to open the new strawberry seed packet carefully this time. One by one she nestled the seeds in the earth, delicately covered them and brushed the dirt off her lap.

"It's not so hard, is it?" she said to Holly, who was painfully trying to cover her seeds without actually touching the earth so she wouldn't get dirty.

"I wouldn't say that!" Holly giggled.

* * *

Felicity got up and wandered over to get a glass of lemonade. Planting was thirsty work.

Refreshed, she skipped back to her patch and chose another packet of seeds.

"Raspberries this time," she thought. "Now where did I plant those strawberries?" Closing her eyes and making a guess with her wand, Felicity began to make more rows

"Oh no!" she said as she discovered a seed with her wand. "Now, is that a spilt strawberry seed? Oh well, plants must need friends just like everyone else and there's nothing wrong with being cosy. I'll plant the raspberries here too!"

* * *

It had been a hard afternoon's work, but finally the fairies had planted and watered all the seeds that Daisy and Felicity had selected that morning.

"Has anyone seen my wand?" said Felicity, dashing around frantically. "I have a nasty feeling I may have planted it."

"It's in your pocket!" said Holly, looking up at the sky in despair.

"Phew," said Felicity. "But it might

have been nice to see what would
have happened if I had buried it.
I wonder if it would have turned into
a wand tree..."

With all the fairies gathered round,
Daisy stood up and explained that
there was only one thing left to do
before they left their seeds to grow.

"Are you sure we really need to talk
to our seeds?" said Felicity, amused.

"If you don't they won't grow big
and strong," said Daisy earnestly.
"Seeds are little living things, just
like you and me. They need
encouragement to grow."

"I couldn't possibly talk to my
seeds!" said Holly. "Someone might
see me – it's bad enough having to
wear gardening gloves that don't
match!"

"Well, it's up to you," said Daisy. "Organic gardening means not using any artificial chemicals to make the plants grow, so they need all the help they can get."

Holly considered this for a moment, and looked at Polly, who had already got up to go and chat to her patch.

"OK," Holly said, "but don't you dare tell anyone!"

✳ ✳ ✳

Over the next few weeks, Felicity, Holly and Polly met regularly after school to watch the progress of their organic garden and, at the insistence of Daisy, whisper words of encouragement to the tiny sprouts that had begun to peep through the earth.

It was like magic. Soon everyone's patch showed neat little rows of green leaves, all except for Felicity's patch, which was fast becoming a jungle!

"I don't understand," said Daisy, scratching her head. "You made such neat little rows when you planted your seeds."

"I know," said Felicity agreeing awkwardly, having realised her mistake. "Strange, isn't it?"

"What did you plant? I can't see your markers," Daisy asked.

"Oh, I didn't use any markers; I thought I'd remember what I planted. But I've forgotten!"

Daisy just sighed and shook her head.

"Surprises are always nice!" said Felicity cheerfully.

* * *

As the weeks went on the plants got taller and stronger. Polly's mint was almost ready to pick, Holly's tomatoes were turning cherry red, Daisy's blackberries were ripening... and Felicity's jungle got bigger. Just another few days and they would be able to have their own home-grown organic feast.

* * *

It was mid-week after ballet class that they discovered their garden had visitors.

"Caterpillars!" squealed Holly, aghast.

"Big green ones!" shrieked Polly.

"They're creepy-crawlies," cried

Felicity, flying high away from the danger zone.

"Well," said Daisy. "In proper organic gardening you mustn't use chemical insect killer to protect your plants, and I'm afraid I don't know of any alternative. These look like very hungry caterpillars. We'll just have to hope they leave some for us!"

* * *

At school the next day Holly, Polly, Daisy and Felicity met under the large oak in the playing field at lunch time to plan their organic feast.

"Well, we can start with some salad using Daisy's lettuce and my tomatoes," suggested Holly, making a list in her notebook.

"And I'll make some mint dressing!" said Polly.

"Then we can have hot jacket potatoes," said Holly, drawing a little picture on her notes.

"And Felicity's strawberries for pudding!" said Daisy. "It will be perfect."

* * *

The organic feast day arrived. Polly and Daisy carefully picked all the vegetables, and Felicity and Holly washed and prepared them. It all looked scrummy and made such a difference to know that they had grown them all from seed themselves.

Daisy set up her favourite garden
furniture in front of their organic
plots and laid the table with her best
rose-print china.

"I wish we had some flowers for
the table," said Daisy as she sat
down to join the others for the feast.
"I've been so busy with the organic
fruit and vegetables I'd forgotten the
rest of the garden. It's usually so
colourful."

Just then the air was filled
with a soft fluttering noise
and the sky burst into a
thousand tiny patches of
beautiful colours.

"Butterflies!" the
fairies gasped, looking
up in awe as a hundred
rainbow wings took flight.
"Isn't gardening pure
fairy magic?" said Felicity,
smiling her biggest smile ever.
"Holly's seeds have turned
into these bursting red
tomatoes, Polly's
planting has produced
lots of marvellously
minty things, Daisy's
dedication and tiniest
seeds have created the most
enormous blackberries ever,
my strawberries are just delicious...

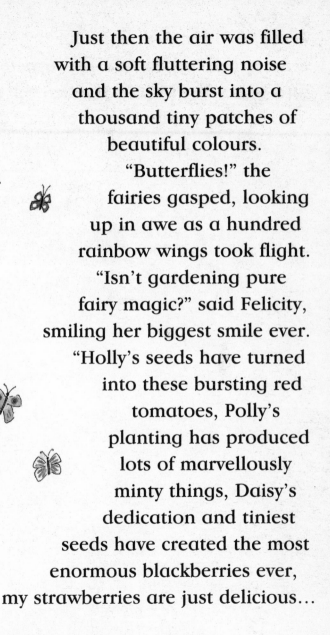

51

And who'd have thought our organic-fed caterpillars would have turned into butterflies that have filled the sky with a dazzling display of colour!"

The magic of
nature is

that it is full
of unexpected
surprises

Clutter Clean-out

Felicity Wishes smoothed down the folds in her skirt as she looked in the mirror.

"There," she said with satisfaction, turning round and looking at her reflection over her shoulder. It had taken her ages to decide what to wear but finally she looked just right.

"Thank goodness, I'm already late meeting Holly, Polly and Daisy at Sparkles," thought Felicity, desperately trying to find her wings.

She glanced round the room at the clothes scattered across the floor. She had practically emptied her wardrobe in her search for the perfect outfit. Hurriedly she tried to put things back in her wardrobe. But no matter how much she pushed and shoved, it still wouldn't close.

"I'll just have to do it later," she thought, leaving a huge pile of clothes in the middle of her bedroom floor.

When Felicity arrived at Sparkles, the café on the corner, the other fairies were already on their second milkshakes.

"Where have you been?" asked Holly curiously. "We were starting to worry about you."

"I couldn't close my wardrobe door. I think I may have too many clothes."

The other fairies laughed.

"Of course you do," said Polly affectionately. "Perhaps you should get rid of some of them," she said, pushing a strawberry milkshake towards Felicity.

"I really don't like the idea of throwing my clothes away. It seems such a waste," said Felicity slurping.

"You don't have to throw them away," offered Daisy. "You could take them to the charity shop."

"And I've got piles of hair-spray cans and make-up bottles that need recycling. Do you think the charity shop will want them too?" interrupted Holly.

"And I never know what to do with all my old toothpaste boxes. Do you think they would take them?" said

Polly, who wanted to be a Tooth Fairy when she graduated from fairy school.

"Maybe not," said Daisy, looking puzzled. "But there must be other ways to recycle our old stuff to help cut down on waste. We just need to think a little creatively."

The fairies thought long and hard. Suddenly Felicity had a brain-wave!

"I know," squealed Felicity. "Why don't I throw a clothes swapping party at my house? Everyone can exchange their old clothes for each other's cast-offs."

"That's a great idea," said Polly, nearly pinging off her chair with excitement.

* * *

The next day Holly, Polly and Daisy arrived at Felicity's house even before the Post Fairy had delivered the mail. They each had a large bag of clothes they wanted to swap.

Each of the fairies tipped the contents of their bags on to Felicity's heap in the middle of her bedroom floor. It looked like a patchwork mountain!

"What in fairy world have you got there?" asked Holly, prodding Felicity's old green cardigan. Lifting it up with the end of her wand, she looked at it with eyebrows raised. "It's not very 'you'!" she said.

"Well, it was a bit of an impulse choice," admitted Felicity, blushing.

* * *

Soon socks, tights and old dresses were flying back and forth through the air as the fairies dived into the pile of clothes. Even Holly thought she might find something useful.

"OK," said Holly, picking up the ugly green cardigan for the third time. "We need a system!"

"Why don't we sort this lot out into piles?" offered Polly, the sensible fairy in the group. Polly sorted three main categories of clothes: swapping clothes, charity shop clothes, and dusters clothes (which were far too old for any self-respecting fairy to be seen in!).

"This is not only a great way to recycle," said Felicity beaming, "it's also a great way to sort out our wardrobes too. Mine was in a desperate need of a tidy." Felicity always aspired to being tidy like Polly, but somehow she always ended up with messy cupboards.

By the end of the afternoon everything was sorted, swapped and cut up. The four fairy friends were exhausted but thrilled with all the new clothes they had for their wardrobes.

"I'm so pooped I can barely wiggle my wings," said Felicity yawning. "Why don't I take what's left here to the charity shop and I'll meet you tomorrow in Sparkles for an extra special strawberry milkshake!" Holly, Polly and Daisy readily agreed.

* * *

Refreshed after their good night's sleep, the fairies were full of energy when they met up again the next morning – each wearing a cast-off item from each other's wardrobe!

"Shall we start at my house today?" asked Holly, who was keen to make the most of everyone's enthusiasm before it ran out.

When the fairies arrived at Holly's  house they discovered piles and piles of old make-up pots, shampoo bottles and hair-spray cans in the corner of her bathroom.

"What shall I do with it all?" despaired Holly.

"Hmm," said Felicity thinking hard. Felicity was always eager to help her friends in any way she could and scanned the room for inspiration. "You could make a shampoo bottle and hair-spray can sculpture? Or... lipstick earrings?" she suggested as she spied Holly's make-up box. "Hair-spray can bookends?" she

mused, looking at the bookshelves.
"Face cream pot vases?"

All her ideas seemed silly and she
was just about to give up when she
had a flash of inspiration. "Christmas
tree decorations from old bottles and
pots?"

"Perfect!" said Holly.
"Felicity, you're a genius!"
Felicity's cheeks turned
a deep shade of pink.
Holly desperately wanted

to be a Christmas Fairy when she
graduated from the School of Nine
Wishes and this was a great way to
show Fairy Godmother that she was
taking her chosen career seriously.

"Of course!" laughed Polly. "We
can paint these bottle tops pretty
festive colours and give them
a special sparkly
touch!"

"And we can add tiny bells to these containers to make them jingle," offered Holly.

"That sounds like fun. Let's start now!" said Daisy excitedly.

The fairies spent a very creative day cutting and painting, sticking on ribbons and glitter, and making all sorts of beautiful and unusual festive decorations. When they'd finished, Holly was delighted with the decorations and could hardly wait for Christmas, which was months away!

* * *

After a lunchtime treat of sticky buns and yummy chocolate cookies,

66

Felicity and her friends flew over to Daisy's house.

"What can we recycle of yours, Daisy?" asked Felicity. After their morning of successful recycling, Felicity was confident that they would be able to sort out Daisy's bits and pieces. Daisy went quiet.

"Well, Daisy?" asked Holly curiously. "You haven't told us what you want to recycle."

"Erm, well, I need to do something with all the bits and pieces left over from my garden. It seems mad to be throwing it away when I'm trying to be green with my organic gardening."

"Don't worry, we are happy to help whatever the job," said Felicity confidently.

Daisy smiled hesitantly at the other fairies. "Basically, I need a compost heap," she said quickly and under her breath.

"What! Ugh! No way!" squealed Holly in disgust. "I'm not going to get my wand dirty in a big pile of horrible, smelly stuff!"

Polly wasn't convinced either. "Daisy, I've suddenly remembered. I need to return my copy of 'Toothy Tales' to the library today," she said sheepishly. "I'm not sure when the library shuts but I'd better be getting back..."

"Don't worry, I don't expect you to be handling the rubbish itself," explained Daisy, laughing at the fairies' wrinkled noses. "I just need to build a wooden box that I can fill with my grass clippings, old leaves and twigs. In a few months it will be compost and I can spread it on my organic garden. The plants will love it!"

Daisy's enthusiasm was beginning to rub off on the others.

"So we don't have to actually touch anything smelly?" asked Holly, slightly reassured.

"No, we just need some wood and nails," said Daisy cheerfully.

Felicity's relief was obvious. "Fantastic! Sounds great! Where shall we start?"

The fairies spent a few hours nailing together planks of wood to make the compost heap. When they finished, they stood back and admired their handiwork.

"Phew, that was hard work!" said Felicity, wiping her brow.

"Thank you all so much!" said Daisy, clapping her hands together. "It's going to make such a difference. Now I'm doing my bit for the environment too!" Daisy was so delighted with her compost container that she made a scrummy jug of ice-cold lemonade for her friends.

"Well, that's recycling problems solved for me, Holly and Daisy."

Felicity took a sip of lemonade. "Now we just have to sort things out for you, Polly. Shall we come over tomorrow? I'm sure it won't take long; we're getting rather good at it now. I think green might just be the new pink!"

* * *

The following day, Felicity arrived at Polly's house to find Holly, Polly and Daisy staring curiously into a bag.

"What's the matter?" Felicity asked.

"We're trying to think of something different to do with used tooth boxes," explained Daisy, frowning.

"Hmm, that's a bit more difficult than Holly and Daisy's rubbish," said Felicity, peering into the bag Holly was holding. "I guess we can't refill them..."

"And they won't make very good decorations…" added Holly.

The fairies racked their brains for something creative to do.

"It's no good," said Polly sadly. "We're going to have to throw these away."

"No, we're not," said Felicity, refusing to admit defeat. The other fairies looked hopefully at their

friend. "In this morning's edition of *The Daily Flutter*, they announced the opening of a new recycling centre in Little Blossoming. They recycle everything from plastics to paper to cans and bottles."

"That's a great idea, Felicity," said Polly, delighted. She hadn't wanted to be the only fairy who hadn't found a way to do her bit for the environment.

When they got to the centre it was actually more fun than Felicity had imagined.

Closing their eyes, the fairies counted the seconds before the tooth boxes crashed into the cardboard pile inside the large green container.

With a job well done, the satisfied fairies flew to Felicity's house to put their feet up with a creamy hot chocolate.

"What a busy couple of days!" said Daisy, barely able to keep her eyelids open. "I'm exhausted."

"I never realised there were so man
small ways to help the environment,"
said Felicity, eyeing up the last
marshmallows on the plate. "If no one
is going to eat those, I'm sure I can
think of a way to
recycle them."
But Holly, Polly
and Daisy
dived at the
plate before
Felicity had
a chance to even reach out for them.

"How environmentally friendly we
all are!" laughed Felicity as she
watched her friends munching
happily.

"You know what they say, practice makes perfect!" and she opened another bag!

Magical transformations

mean everything gets
a second chance

If you enjoyed this book, why not
try another of these fantastic
story collections?

Clutter Clean-out

Designer Drama

Newspaper Nerves

Star Surprise

Also available in the Felicity Wishes range:

Felicity Wishes: Snowflakes and Sparkledust

It is time for spring to arrive in Little Blossoming but there is a problem and winter is staying put. Can Felicity Wishes get the seasons back on track?

Felicity Wishes: Secrets and Surprises

Felicity Wishes is planning her birthday party but it seems none of her friends can come. Will Felicity end up celebrating her birthday alone?

Felicity Wishes has lots to say in these fantastic little books:

Little Book of Love

Little Book of Peace

Little Book of Hiccups

Little Book of Every Day Wishes

Little Book of Fun